The Firekeeper's Son

The Firekeeper's Son

by LINDA SUE PARK

Illustrated by JULIE DOWNING

CLARION BOOKS

New York

Clarion Books
a Houghton Mifflin Company imprint
215 Park Avenue South, New York, NY 10003
Text copyright © 2004 by Linda Sue Park
Illustrations copyright © 2004 by Julie Downing

The illustrations were executed in watercolor and pastel.
The text was set in 16-point Tiepolo Bold.

www.houghtonmifflinbooks.com

Printed in Singapore.

Library of Congress Cataloging-in-Publication Data
Park, Linda Sue.
The firekeeper's son / by Linda Sue Park ; illustrated by Julie Downing.
p. cm.
Summary: In early-19th-century Korea, after Sang-hee's father injures his ankle,
Sang-hee attempts to take over the task of lighting the evening fire,
which signals to the palace that all is well. Includes historical notes.
ISBN 0-618-13337-2 (alk. paper)
[1. Signals and signaling—Fiction. 2. Fire—Fiction.
3. Korea—History—19th century—Fiction.]
I. Downing, Julie, ill. II. Title.
PZ7.P22115 Fi 2003
[E]—dc21   2002013917

TWP 10 9 8 7 6 5 4 3 2 1

To Julie, sister and friend
—L. S. P.

To Ashley, Dwight, Martha, Mira, and Susan,
my guides in art and life
—J. D.

"We live in an important village," Sang-hee's father said.

Sang-hee looked around.
A few huts made of wood and mud.
A few cows.
A few chickens, a few dogs.
It did not look like an important village.

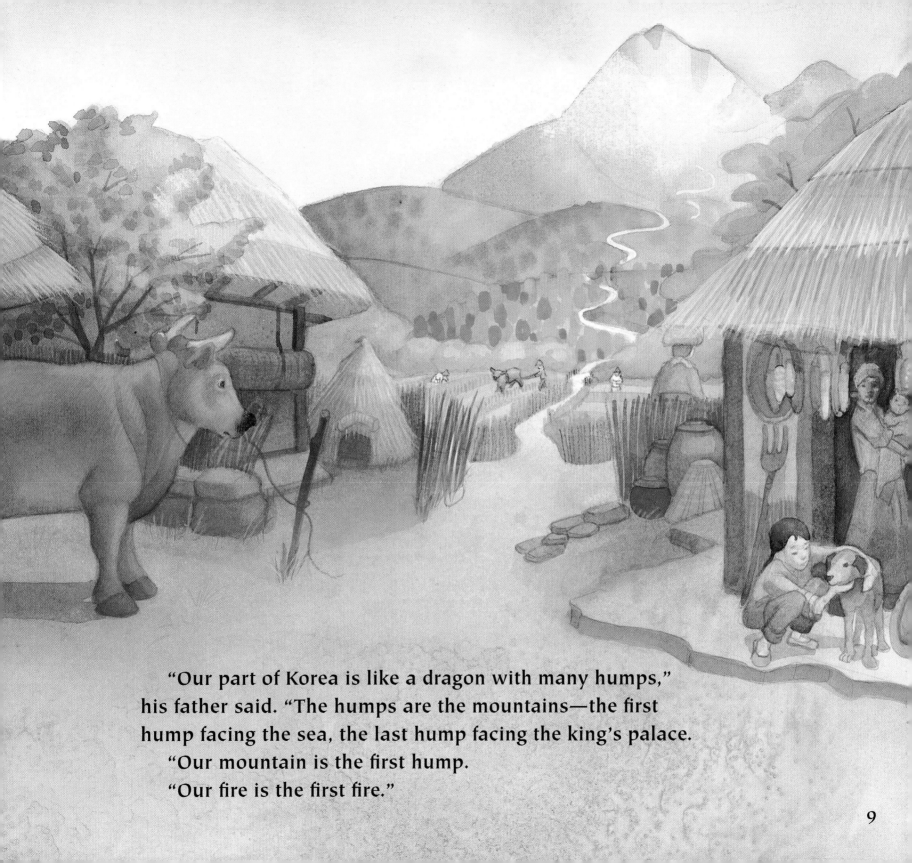

"Our part of Korea is like a dragon with many humps,"
his father said. "The humps are the mountains—the first
hump facing the sea, the last hump facing the king's palace.

"Our mountain is the first hump.

"Our fire is the first fire."

9

Every evening at sunset Sang-hee's father climbed to the top of the mountain carrying a pair of tongs and a little brass pot filled with live coals.

Coals to start a fire.

A fire so big it could be seen from the next mountain.

Where another firekeeper saw it and lit *his* fire. A fire big enough to be seen from the *next* mountain.

Where a third firekeeper saw it. And lit *his* fire.

And on and on.

A fire on every hump of the dragon's back, all the way to the last one—the hump that could be seen from the palace walls.

When the king saw the fire on the last mountain, he knew that all was well in the land.

"When trouble comes to our land, it almost always comes from the sea," Sang-hee's father explained. "If ever we see enemy ships, I will not light our fire. And the next firekeeper will not light *his* fire. And on and on, until the king sees only darkness on the last hump. He will know that trouble has come to our land, and he will send soldiers to fight the enemy.

"We are fortunate," Sang-hee's father said. "In your time, and my time, and your grandfather's time, the fire has always been lit.

"It is good to live in a time of peace.

"It is good that soldiers have never come."

Soldiers!
Tall, brave soldiers.
With shining swords.
Sang-hee wished he could see soldiers.
Just once.

Evening.

Sang-hee shooed the chickens into their coop. He glanced up at the mountain, looking for the fire.

No fire. His father was a little late.

Sang-hee fetched water from the river. He poured the water into the barrel, then glanced up the mountain again.

No fire.

Sang-hee looked out at the sea, where the setting sun made a path on the water.

Could those be ships bobbing on the waves?

No. Just a flock of seagulls.

No enemies.

No trouble.

But still no fire.

17

Sang-hee called his mother. He pointed at the mountain.
She looked, then turned and stared at the sea. "Sang-hee,
you must run and see what has happened," she said.
"Something is wrong—there is no trouble from the sea,
and the fire must be lit!"

Sang-hee ran up the mountain path. He knew
the path like a friend.
But tonight it was not at all friendly.
Stones tripped him.
Branches reached out to lash at his face.
He ran until he could not run anymore.

A strange noise—a groaning sound.
A groan from the bushes by the path.
"Father!"
"Sang-hee, I am all right. But I fell and hurt my ankle, and I fear
it is broken. I cannot walk. You must light the fire. Hurry!"

Sang-hee grabbed the brass pot and ran again.
The fire—he had to light the fire!
His feet pounded out a song on the path—*light the fire,*
light the fire, light the fire . . .

At last Sang-hee reached the top of the mountain.
There was the brush pile, ready to be lit. He knelt,
trembling from his run. He picked up one coal with
the tongs—and dropped it.

It broke into a hundred red jewels that glowed for
a moment, then died.

A second coal.

Gleaming bright as . . . as a soldier's sword.

If there is no fire, the soldiers will come. They will be angry when they find no enemies here.

But maybe—maybe not all of them will be angry.

Maybe there is a soldier who would be glad for a chance to visit the sea.

I could show him the beach.
Where to catch the best fish.
Where to find the prettiest shells.
After that he might teach me a little about sword-fighting . . .

27

Sang-hee wished he could see soldiers.

Just once.

I could say I dropped the pot. And spilled all the coals. That it was an accident.

While Sang-hee thought, the second coal burned out.

He looked into the brass pot.

Only one coal left.

One coal, glowing fiercely. Almost as if it were talking.

As if it were saying, *Light the fire, light the fire . . .*

And *A time of peace, a time of peace . . .*

In his father's voice.